DAVID RU GW01398789

SERIES

TRANNY'S ON A PLANE
&
TRANNY'S ON A TRAIN

By Jimmy Swagger

To request permission, contact Jimmy Swagger at jimmy@jimmyswagger.com

Cover design by Evelyn Raph
Interior formatting by Josh
Published by: Miss Lacy Publishing

DEDICATION

This one's for you, Stephanie, my rock through all of this crazy ride.

To my crew: Josh, couldn't have done this without your sharp editing, killer formatting, and that slick interior design.

Evelyn, your cover art was straight fire!

Camille, Sebastian, Eric, Joseph, Isiah, Tony, K2, Diego, Spencer and Raymond Sr. and Jr., y'all have been legends.

And a shoutout to all my amigos holding it down in federal and state prison. This one's for you too.

Lucas Marcus, you're part of the family, man.

Thanks for the support, for the laughs, and for always having my back.

Table of Contents

TRANNY'S ON A PLANE

1. "BOARDING PASS"

I handed Jesse my boarding pass. She took the check-in tag and started typing on her computer. She was a really cute Latina girl. I was catching a flight from LAX to Berlin. She handed my tickets back and told me my flight would board in 25 minutes, with a nice, beautiful grin! I thanked her and had a seat.

As I was going through my emails, I saw a message from my publisher. She informed me we had some bites from two big boys on a nice deal for my new manuscript. It was a murder, psycho thriller.

I was heading to Berlin to meet with a company that was interested in my new invention. I had acquired a patent and was trying to license it.

God knows I could use the cash. I had recently made some poor business decisions, so my life was at a low point. I had to sell my Chevrolet just to afford this trip! Hey, it was a Hail Mary, but at worst, I was going to have some nice German beers and maybe meet a cute German girl!

"Flight 1013 from LAX to Berlin now boarding. Thank you for choosing Cloudy Skies Airlines," said Jesse over the intercom.

I gathered up my luggage and got in line.

2. "BAD ASS BITCH"

As I was heading down the skybridge, this 6'6" badass Russian bitch was bouncing the skybridge like a trampoline. It reminded me of a trampoline birthday party when I was 6.

It was at this boy's house, a rich kid's house, Danny, I think his name was. Every bit of 200 pounds. I mean, this kid's parents had to have him on a steady diet of Snickers, Cheetos and soda pop. He hopped on the trampoline and the girls were the first to go!

Shamu was present! Well, I figured this was a good time to give my triple ganor a try. What could go wrong here? This kid was the fulcrum the Egyptians used to build the pyramids! He was getting me 20 feet in the air!

Well, 20 stitches later, I found out that was a terrible IDEA!

I managed to keep my balance walking to the airlock and was greeted by Stevie. That's what his Cloudy Skies name tag read. "Row 21, aisle seat, Mr. Rutherford." I swear he winked at me.

I made my way to seat 21A. I was trying to squeeze my bag in the overhead compartment when that huge Russian bitch grabbed my bag, stuffed it in all grunting and shit. WTF? I turned face first into the ugliest rack I had ever witnessed! Well, et's just say I stepped aside.

3. "GOTTA SHIT BAD"

I was just getting comfortable when "Ivan the Terrible" wanted to get up. Well, it was not a choice; she just moved across me. I swear, as I was wiggling out, a ballsack rubbed my arm. I stood up, and my arm smelled like a mix of sweaty balls and a bar chick's breath, the one you just cannot get away from.

As I looked around, I noticed that all the Russian beasts were gone. Had to be a Russian polka dance contest in Berlin.

As I sat back down, my stomach went whoomp...grrlt.... Damn! I knew that stop at Taco Bell was a bad idea before an international flight! Fuck!

Well, as I made my way to the back of this enormous international Flight 1013 aircraft, all the toilets were occupied. I waited 10 minutes, then as that turtle head started to poke out, I seriously had to make a move.
There were more toilets down below!

As I headed back through the redneck screaming babies, curry-scented chefs, Japanese tourists, and plushietossing teenagers, each step to that stairwell was extremely dangerous!

4. "TOILET PLAYBOY"

I made it downstairs. Now it was a lengthy sprint, and that beautiful stewardess was in the aisle. Stevie was in the other one. This was a no-brainer. As I got to Jessica, she saw me shuffling towards her and had a magazine and scotch in hand! I seriously was in love, if it wasn't for that turtle giving birth out of my ass! I waddled and moved as fast as I could.

I flung that door open, almost spilling my drink, made it in a hover, then splat...thunk, midair deposit! That was close!

5. "BIDET GONE ALL WRONG"

Hustler! Good shit. I'll be a motherfucker. A scotch, Hustler, and a good Taco Bell shit! The only thing missing was actual pussy. I was thumbing through, grabbed the scotch, bottoms up...literally.

At that moment, a note fell out.

"Mr. Rutherford, I am a super fan of your books! Miss Lacy was a great take on a mix of female intimacy, horror, and sexual freedom! I'll knock on your door at
10:35!"

P.S. I want you to fuck my brains out!
XOXO, Jesse

Fuck, it was 10:33 and there was no toilet paper?! Fuck! Fuck me! Guess Mrs. April is going to have to work. Shit a button! As I pressed it, water went everywhere...Fuck!

About that time...knock...knock softly. I grabbed my T-shirt, wiped my ass, and stuffed that thing down the toilet. "Hang on," I yelled. I washed my hands and opened the door.

It was Jesse with a bottle of scotch and a pack of cigarettes! Like I said, I was in love! She asked about my shirt, "Don't ask," I replied. She popped that skirt's button, like a size 36 on a fat boy's 42 waist. OMG, fuck yea, red lace. We turned up that bottle and I spun her around and went "Cock Lesnar" on her ass. I fucked her like she was the last woman on earth! After we ripped that smoke detector down and had a couple camels, it couldn't have smelled any worse than the curry chefs.

She said, "Hold on, I'll get a shirt from Stevie." At that moment, we heard screams.

6. "TRANNY'S GO LOCO"

As I looked out the restroom door, it was...

"Those mother fuckin trannys takin the plane!"

Jesse tapped my shoulder. "What's going on?" she asked. "Shhh, it's those ugly ass Russian broads," I told her. I looked over; it was the galley. "Does the galley have a dumbwaiter elevator?" "Actually, it does. It leads to the belly of the plane," she said. We devised a plan to crawl to the galley.

Okay, this shit was about to go off the chains! Halfnaked author "David Rutherford," a hot-ass stewardess,
"Jesse Martinez" AKA Latin Beauty! What could go wrong...Oh yeah, we could be killed by

"The mother fuckin trannys on the plane!"

So I opened the door. The furthest tranny from us had "Stevie Thompson" hostage. He was definitely going drama queen. Drama queen, not drag queen, although maybe? If they let him go, he would go Ru Paul in here!

So Jesse and I scurried across the aisle to the galley. Fucking Jesse knocked some shit off the counter...clunk...loud as FUCK! I peeked around the corner. Fuck, here came a Russian princess with a fucking machine gun. I stuffed Jesse in the elevator and hit the button. Fuck, that thing's noisy!

Shit...Shit...I looked all around, no fucking cabinets. The only place to hide was in the dumbwaiter shaft! I looked for some sort of weapons. Nothing but paper soybean-based sporks and straws! Fuck green peace.

Right now I sure wish I had finished those martial arts classes. I fucked off and joined just to meet a spandexwearing girl in my complex, then dropped out thinking, when will I ever need to know this shit?

Well, the tranny was 10, plus or minus, feet away, so I hopped in. Please, God, keep walking. I was at this point wishing I was able to do Jedi mind tricks! Wave my hand, "It was a raccoon...nothing to see here, walk away."

I could see his silhouette. He yelled something in Russian, and then walked away! Fucking close.

7. "THE LUGGAGE HOOK-UP"

I poked my head out... All clear. What the fuck was going on? I was glad as fuck I had tucked that bottle of scotch and cigarettes in my pants. I hit the button and got in the elevator. As it stopped, Jesse ran up. "Oh, thank God, David!" Jesse said all in a panic. "I thought they had captured you!" "What are we going to do?" she asked.

Hmmmm... That red lace was popping out; I had a few ideas! Well, when in Rome... was my first thought. I mean, this could be my last day alive! They say danger is a turn on! I pulled her in tight. "Don't worry, kitten, we are going to finish this scotch, fuck, and get the fuck off this plane!" You could tell her panties instantly got wet! Yep, daddy was about to take care of business. She grabbed that bottle and drank half of it in a single swig. Hell yeah, I loved this woman! She passed me the bottle, had my pants down before I turned it up! She sucked my cock like it had never been sucked before! We fucked probably the rest of the way over Russia.

8. "TIME TO FUCK A TRANNY"

Well, good times don't last forever. It was time to go Harrison Ford on these wanna be lesbians. I got up halfcocked still and told Jesse, "Let's search luggage."

We started to peel bags open. I found some night vision goggles, really?! Who the fuck was on this plane, Rambo? In that same suitcase, a 9mm, all in pieces, some ammo, an axe, and a flak jacket?! Seriously?!

In another bag, I found a paintball gun and tons of paintballs. I mean, I can't even get a Sprite past TSA, WTF?! Also found a lot of drugs! Cocaine, some meth, weed, and at least 6 bottles of various booze! Do those scanners even work??

Jesse came over with 2 pocket knives, 4 cans of hairspray, 2 lighters, and a slingshot. She was my girl! We are definitely trading numbers, emails, and Facebooks. I told her to climb through that service panel and see if they had a communication section in the nose of the plane like I saw once in a movie.

About 20 minutes went by, and she poked her head out.

9. "COMMUNICATION MISSION"

"I found a server bank, it's got a laptop. I was able to log in and get an email out about the hijacking of Flight 1013," said Jesse.

I told her to hang out there; I was going to try to take the lower deck back. She replied, "Let's just grab the booze and hang out, David. You're not Commando." Well, it was a nice thought, but she was 100% correct! She didn't have to twist my arm. I fed up our stash and climbed my ass in that little access panel.

As we were chillin', drinking, fucking, doing some coke, and smoking some weed, we heard some yelling.
Fuck!

10. "RATS DISCOVERED"

Well, so much for chillin' till the cavalry comes. I was getting fond of Jesse, so I guess it's time to "John Wayne" it and save the plane. I climbed up and looked out the panel. It was the fuckin' trannies; they had discovered someone was loose, and they did not look happy. There was a trapdoor with a ladder, and one disappeared up it.

I went back and told Jesse, "Well, either we take this tranny, or they're going to discover our hideout!" She agreed, "What now, David?" Hmmm, that was a fuckin' good question. I suited up, put everything in a duffle bag, and said, "Fuck it."

As I got to the access panel, they had a tranny posted at the ladder. I had to do something to distract him. I remembered there were a couple of oxygen masks in the server room. I went back and told Jesse to see what she could find in the computer to kill the plane's climate control, as I looked around.

As I was looking, I found another room. It was the service room for all the oxygen on the plane for cabin pressurizing. Fuck yea. I was a 30-year engineer before writing books, so I had extensive knowledge here. I went back, and Jesse said she found the electrical controls in there and emergency beacon activation. Bingo! Well, it was a weak plan, but a plan. I kissed my future wife and told her to wait to kill the lights till the plane started to decrease altitude, cause loss of cabin pressure, then hope like hell.

11. "I LOVE IT WHEN A PLAN COMES TOGETHER!"

As I went to the service access to cut the oxygen for cabin pressure, I grabbed the duffle bag and night vision goggles. I really had to find the Rambo this shit belonged to. I got to the access hatch and waited. Almost 10 minutes to the second, the plane started to decrease in altitude. On point, Jesse hit the power. The plane started to dive. Go time!

I hopped out, took the taser, and shot the motherfuckin' tranny right between the eyes. Fucking tranny's eyes glowed? Crazy! About that time, the radio squelched with no response; they would know their pests were in luggage. I hid behind some crates and waited.

As soon as tranny #2 opened the hatch and started down the ladder, I popped off 4 shots, and he dropped. As I made it over, I couldn't help myself, "Yippie ki ya, motherfucker!" I put 3 in his head. Tranny #3 shut the hatch.

Fuck, now I was in a stalemate. Guess I had to wait it out. I was straight pulling from Die Hard. Grabbed the radio, "I got two Russian princesses down here, one with scrambled eggs for a brain, the other with 3 slugs in his forehead." A few seconds passed, then...

"So who do I have the pleasure of talking to?" I swear it sounded just like Lars from the movie, WTF? "I'm the guy who's about to kill all your men, you Russian piece of shit!" I said. "Ahh, a true hero, American I presume? A John Wayne?" Okay, he was educated; these trannies were as dumb as hell, not him. What the fuck was going on? This was more than a hijacking. I needed to antagonize this jackass. What were his plans? "So, John Wayne, what rock did you crawl out from?" Lars said. "The rock I'm going to bash your face in shortly with!" I told him. "Ahh, I see. Well, these passengers are all paid for, John Wayne," Lars continued. Fuck, I'm in some Hostel movie now. Shit just went from reverse to first gear. I had to get this plane back and win the girl!

12. "A RE-HIJACKING"

About that time, the hatch opened. "Hey," okay, that motherfucker almost became the poster child for "your brain on drugs." "Hey, we took out the Russian lady," the man said down the hatch. Fuck yea, now we had a posse! I climbed up. "Anyone else knows how to use a gun?" I asked. "I do," The guy said. I had to ask, "You must be the 9mm, night vision goggles, battle ax guy?" *I said.* "Yea, how did you know?" The guy asked. I opened the duffle bag and handed him his shit. Yep, we had a soldier now. Time to re-hijack this fuckin' plane!

Well, the guy gave these two dudes a machine gun and gave them a quick lesson. Wasn't much, but they were down to 3 men. We had the numbers.

"Does anyone have any piloting experience?" I asked, cause in every movie, someone always kills the only man who can fly the fucker. Then it's some bullshit miraculous landing with some cheesedick tower guy sweating, followed by a round of applause! That's only in Hollywood! In real life, you need a real fucking pilot.

"I do," said an 80-year-old guy. Hmmm, a WWII plane maybe? This was a commercial airliner. "Well, welcome to Cloudy Skies! What's the name, Captain?" "Johnny; Johnny Skybright..." I almost fell out. I am totally writing a novel on this shit! You cannot make this up...Johnny Skybright?!

13. "DINNER PLANS"

I grew up in Arkansas, yea go ahead with the hillbilly jokes. Seriously though, they had a saying in the deep South, "I'm here to fuck up one of two things: steers and queers. Looks like we were fresh out of steers!" Yep, the 5 of us had dinner plans. A fresh, cold plate of revenge!

We decided to clear the lower level first, then make our way up to the 2nd deck. Man, I had to shit like a motherfucker. "Hang on, guys!" I said, ditching out to the toilet. This time, I took some paper towels from the galley.

That Taco Bell was going 10 rounds with me.

Ahh, I also snuck that tray with the mini shooters. Fuck yea, Lemon Drops! Well, after my meteorite deposit and 6 shooters, I was ready to do this. "Take left, we'll take right," said Gunny. Well, if you need to hand off the reins, who better than a Marine!

The passengers looked terrified and happy as fuck at the same time to see us. I got to Stevie and told him to gather the passengers and take them to the lower luggage compartment. Stevie winked and kissed me on the cheek.

We started peeling the passengers back like a scene from *Black Hawk Down*. We got midway when tranny #4 started screaming some shit on the radio in Russian to Lars. Gunny got low with his ax.

This motherfucker snuck up and buried that hatchet in his forehead like William Wallace in *Braveheart*. Hell yea, thank God for the U.S. Marines!! Tranny #4 was a Black Hawk Down! The passengers cheered! I told them to go with Stevie. Fuck, we had a real chance here. We had 6 a.m. dinner plans, and a tranny pilot was the main course.

14. "SCHOOL'S OUT FOR THE SUMMER!"

We all remember that last day of school, watching the clock for 3:30? That's where we were! Gunny rounded us up. He barked out like a drill sergeant, "David, you and Guy #1 will sneak up and cause a diversion. Me and Guy #2 will wait to ambush Tranny #5." I felt like saying, "Yes, sir." Well, what's the worst thing that could happen? Get served up to a body-harvesting enterprise like a 12-piece from KFC?

"First," Gunny said, "David, you gotta take another shit?" Everyone laughed. "No, seriously, smoke 'em if you got 'em." I whipped out that pack of Camels and the rest of those shooters. Everyone took one. We had a military moment like in *Saving Private Ryan*. The only thing missing was a can of rations.

As we smoked, I took Gunny aside. I told him what Lars said. He told me about a Russian mafia tied to the government and politicians that hijacked planes and then claimed they crashed. They sold the women passengers on the black market to Middle Eastern sheiks who liked them young. The rest were sold for body harvesting. So, we had to take back this plane!

Well, recess time was over. Guy #1 and I made our way up the stairwell. I used the "fist" (hold-up) signal. Fuckin' cool! If Jesse could see me now, instant wet panties! I was fuckin' Harrison Ford from *Air Force One* for sure! Commander in Chief!!

We spotted Tranny #5; he was babbling something on the radio in Russian. We moved low and slow. I motioned for Guy #1 to go to the other aisle. I gave him the signal. We both popped up and ran down the stairwell. Tranny #5 followed. Pop...pop...pop, Tranny #5 down!

We told the passengers to follow Guy #1 down to the luggage compartment.

The curry chefs started babbling something in Arabic, seriously? I said, "Do you understand the words coming out of my mouth?" I pointed to the stairs.

Both of the redneck baby daddies wanted to help. I told them to guard the hatch and handed them a couple of the sporks. They looked happy as hell, fuckin' crazy!

I told Gunny we should radio Lars. He agreed. "So, your Russian cunts are all dead but one," I said and waited a few minutes. "So, John Wayne, let's make a deal," Lars said. "I'll let you, your friends, the Marine, and your Latin beauty live. You walk away, I get my plane," Lars said. I paused a moment, then replied, "How about I get these people home, come find you, and bash your head in like I promised." A moment passed. "I have 100 men waiting for this plane on the ground, John Wayne. My offer still stands till then. You have no idea who you're messing with," said Lars. "Fuck off, see you soon," I told him.

15. "CAPTAIN CRUNCH"

I thought, how does he know about me and Jesse? How did he know about Gunny the Marine? He had to be on the plane. A passenger or one of us? We had to act quickly, he was still among us! I'm sure he's armed too!

Gunny said, "We'll handle the pilot's cabin. You take care of our friend Lars." His plan was to use the propane tank to blow the cabin door and take back the plane.

Guy #1and I headed to the luggage compartment to find Lars. As I looked out the window, I saw two Russian MiGs. Fuck, that made things even more complicated.
Gunny needed to handle the pilot quickly!

The clock was ticking and running down fast. We headed to the luggage compartment. When we arrived, Stevie said, "All the passengers are safe and below." I told Guy #1 to stay and watch the hatch. I was going to get Jesse and turn the power back on.

As I approached the server room, Jesse was gone. I searched everywhere, no Jesse. I went back to the luggage compartment and couldn't find her there either. WTF?

Boom, the plane shook! Guess Captain Crunch was the cinnamon in your fuckin' Toast Crunch? The plane started to dive. Fuck! So we were doomed if Johnny Skybright didn't save the day. Hang on...10,000 feet...8,000 feet. I mean, the guy does use a walker...6,000 feet. Ok, the plane started to level out. Whew, we definitely, probably had a good look at the airfield now at this altitude.

16. "THERE'S A SNAKE IN MY BOOT"

Across the radio, Gunny said, "David, get up to the cockpit." I still couldn't find Jesse. I knew if I responded over the radio, it would tip off Lars; *the boss of the Motherfuckin' Trannies on a Plane*. He'd hear and probably kill her! I had to keep this to myself until I figured out what was going on because Lars was on the plane. But who was it? The only person I could trust right now was myself.

Did we just warp into the set of a new "Clue" movie? Or maybe "Scooby-Doo"? Was it the butler, or did Fred just unveil Mr. Wilson?? I had to get to the cockpit. As I climbed up, Guy #1 was gone. WTF? I made my way up to the cockpit and everyone was here. The pilots were both dead! Not a surprise, and tranny #6...was not Lars.

We definitely had a list of issues, besides the fact that there was an unknown psychopath among us. Or that our pilot was in his golden years...20 years ago. Instead of sporting a badass haircut, he was rockin' a pacemaker.

There was an official list:

Problem #1: We were almost out of fuel.

Problem #2: The Russian MiGs would probably shoot us down if we didn't land on the airfield below. Almost certainly bringing a death sentence to 300, give or take, souls.

<u>Problem #3:</u> Guy #1 is super suspect. I mean, he has a terrible haircut. It's always the guy with a terrible haircut. For fuck's sake, the bad guy is always the person with a bad haircut, period!!

<u>Problem #4:</u> By the MiGs outside the window, buzzing us like hornets, this is probably high on the political ranks? I mean, sex slavery or body harvesting to Middle Eastern oil sheiks. That smells of Jeffrey Epstein or the Clintons for sure!

<u>Problem #5:</u> My sex slave, Jesse, is missing.

<u>Problem #6:</u> I really gotta shit again.

<u>Problem #7:</u> The passengers die if we stay in the air, or if we land...unless we find one more movie magic moment like the Golden Ticket from *Last Action Hero*.

<u>Problem #8:</u> There is definitely *a motherfuckin' snake in my boot!*

17. "COCKPIT DRAMA"

I asked Gunny to step aside for a talk. If you're going to "wing" it and trust someone, a Marine is probably the best choice.

As we walked, we discussed the previous list. Yes, I'm an author, so I took the time to write the list and hand it to Gunny. We could scratch off Problem #6: I had to shit...... I wrote that in there. Gunny looked at the list and agreed with all of them. "Okay, ideas?" I asked. He just stood there, blinking.

He had that look you get when you're talking to Jose the landscaper, the one who actually does the work at your house, doesn't speak any English, and you're asking him 100 questions. That look!

Well, WTF? I'm no Bruce Willis, but I had to come up with something, and fast! Maybe go back into the cockpit and play "rock, paper, and scissors"? I needed a speech, a good one, because my plan had an 8% chance of working. I needed an *Independence Day* speech!

I told Gunny, Guy #1, and Guy #2 to meet in the cargo hold, luggage compartment, in 20 minutes. I had an idea. Told Guy #2 to stall the MiGs and O.G., AKA "Johnny," to keep us in the air! Guy #2 gave me the Jose stare. It hit me as I was talking, where was the one place to hide? I thought, *the "Biden Blunder" in Afghanistan—the wheel well!* As far as our DEEP SHIT list, I had a plan. A Hail Mary, Peyton Manning meets Joe Montana try!

As I headed to the luggage compartment, I stopped to talk to Stevie. If there's one person you can trust, it's a pissed-off gay man! I told Stevie, "I need to address the passengers in 20 minutes. Try to get them ready, okay?"

Stevie replied, "Sure thing, Mr. Rutherford." Now, to go find my girl!

Afghanistan? Biden Blunder? Landing gear at the nose! She had to be there! As I climbed down, no tranny #1. He was gone. That had to be Lars. How did we not catch that? I looked around but no Lars. I mean, a 6'6" tranny Russian would have stuck out like an elephant behind a tree!

18. "WHACK A MOLE"

How to find the way to the landing gear? I climbed up to the server room. On the floor lay a dress and wig from *A Motherfuckin' Tranny on a Plane!* And he took all the booze?! That motherfucker! I walked around another access panel—had to be it. I popped it open... and there she was, one pissed-off Latin beauty! I quickly untied her.

"¡Trans pedazo de mierda! ¡Maricón hijo de puta, David, mata ese pinche saco de mierda y mándalo al diablo con el pene en su culo!" she screamed with fiery passion.

I hugged her, and she grabbed my ass so tight I thought she'd rip it off... I love this woman! She was shaken up but okay.

I asked her where the Russian was, and she pointed up to the hatch. I climbed up..... It was the cockpit. And there he was, Mr. Piece of Shit, the one I owed a headbashing to! Right behind me was soon-to-be Mrs. Rutherford. She grabbed my pistol... pop, pop. Lars fell forward... oh shit, the plane was diving. Latin women are all temper! I jumped into the passenger/copilot seat and pulled up to level it out. I hit the autopilot button. Buzzers were going crazy, and Johnny was dead on the floor.

19. "DOWN 17 AND 2 MINUTES ON THE CLOCK"

Well, let's see... no pilot, out of fuel, two Russian fighter jets, and a small army on the ground? Yeah, we're fucked but wait, there's more! Six Ginsu knives and a sharpener! Nah, we're really fucked. I told Jesse, "Wanna go break the news to the folks?" She said, "Yeah, after you fuck me in a pilot's chair!" Oh, I love this girl!! Twenty minutes later...

We got down to the luggage compartment, and I started the "Independence Day" speech. Then I decided, fuck it! I asked everyone else what they wanted to do. We took a vote. 292 to 5 agreed to try to land and fight our way out. Hell yeah!!!

One other guy said he flew a Cessna once. Better than nothing. "Here are the keys, buddy." I had Guy #2 tell the MIGs we were going to land. We gathered everything we could use as weapons and set up. If they were coming in, they were going to have to fight us all!

Our new pilot was Lance-Lance Armstrong. Haha, not fucking with you. What the fuck were his parents thinking? Way fuckin' high!

This was it, 2 minutes left, down by 7. Lance Armstrong at quarterback! He put down the landing gear and started to descend. The passengers buckled in.

You could see the runway, tons of military vehicles. It was do or die! At that very moment... Boom! An explosion to the left. Boom! Explosion to the right. Then, two American fighter jets. Explosions like crazy on the ground! Fuck yeah, the cavalry!

20. "TOUCHDOWN"

The US Air Force! About fuckin' time! The plane erupted in cheers, even the redneck crying babies! But we still weren't out of the woods yet. We had to get this plane on the ground. Man, we needed that tower guy from "Die Hard" like a motherfucker right now!

The pilot "Lance" told everyone to buckle in for a crash landing. I gave Jesse a kiss and sat in the co-pilot's chair. She went back and buckled in. The American fighter jets escorted us as we rounded for approach.

You could see it—the runway. I told Lance, "You got this!" We came down, down, down... ball was in the air... 20, 40, 60 yards! Touchdown... fuck yeah!!!

The plane came to a halt. We slid down, and the Blackhawks were already here! 297 people went up, 297 landed, minus 6...

"Motherfuckin' Tranny's on a Plane!"

CHECK OUT PART TWO

TRANNY'S ON A TRAIN

PART TWO
TRANNY'S ON A TRAIN

1. FUCKED OFF

As I woke up next to Jesse, I realized it was time to move on. Jesse was fun while it lasted, but things were getting too weird. Marriage talk and shit? I'm a 31 flavors Baskin Robbins kind of guy. So I chartered a flight from Berlin to Los Angeles. Time to get fucked off!

I sat Jesse down to tell her it was over...Big mistake. Remember the Latina beauty part? Well, there is another side to that coin....The Latina Diablo side. Let's just say it did not go all too well, to say the least. She went into a RANT!

"Hijo de puta! Yo dejé mi trabajo en 'Cloudy Skys' para ser plantada en Berlin? Fuck you, pedazo de mierda! Te voy a cortar la verga y quitarles el hambre a los cerados y gozar mirando cómo se lo comen. Luego voy a matar y rostizar los lerdos y te los vas a tragar mientras yo me burlo de ti!" Jesse screamed at David.

Well, I really should have paid more attention in Spanish class. I might have seen that empty tequila bottle coming that clocked me right in the chin! I grabbed my bags and booked it!

I am David Rutherford, an author, who just went through a fuckin' tranny experience on a plane. Jesse was a stewardess on the flight. The flight was hijacked by a bunch of Russian trannies, and we ended up taking the plane back. I thought I had won the girl. We narrowly escaped becoming part of a sex trafficking, bodyharvesting Russian gang of:

"Mother Fuckin Tranny's on a Plane!"

2. DALARNA GETS FILLED WITH JOY

As I boarded Flight 999 to Los Angeles from Berlin, my jaw was losing all feeling! But it finally stopped bleeding, somewhat!

When I walked down the aisle, my new stewardess greeted me. Her name tag read "Dalarna." Dalarna...? Sounds like an old 60's song? She was a voluptuous Swedish delight. Yummy...

She took my boarding pass and pointed me to 104B in a very sexy accent. "Are you okay, Mr. Rutherford?" she asked.

"Yes, why?" I responded.

"Your chin is bleeding," she said. "Oh yeah... It's fine, I think," I told her.

"After we take off, I will bandage it for you," said Dalarna.

"Thank you, Dalarna. That would be nice," I told her.

As I went to sit, it was a moment of déjà vu. I went to put my baggage overhead, and the person in 104A was doing the same. It was a schön mädchen, maybe 28 years young. This was going to be a great flight! I could just feel it! 31 Fucking God Damn Flavors!

I grabbed her bags for her after asking and put them overhead. "Danke schön," she said.

"You are welcome," I told her. She offered to sit inside. She had never flown before and really wanted the window seat. I obviously agreed.

As the flight got settled, the little lady next to me offered me a mint. I had to do a breath check... Oh no, I had cat-shit breath? Damn it! It always happens with Taco Bell! I wish I had some Binaca spray. Whatever happened to that shit anyway? Best breath spray ever!

As I went to grab the mint, she dumped 8 in my hand. I must have that hard-to-breathe type of cat-shit breath!

"Are you American?" she asked.
"Yes, David Rutherford," I told her.
"Oh, I know you!" she said.
"Really?" I asked.
She held up a copy of *Miss Lacy*.
"Ahh," I said.
"Suzanna Andstrom," she said.

"Nice to meet you, Suzanna. So, tell me, how is the book? I'm curious. Never really asked anyone," I said.

"Well, to be honest, I really wish you would have gone more into Lacy's past," said Suzanna.

"Oh, just wait, kitten. I'm working on a follow-up novel," I told her.

As I was about to turn up the Mack Daddy charm on Suzanna, over my shoulder... "Mr. Rutherford, would you like me to bandage that chin of yours?" said Dalarna.

"Sure, that would be great!" I told her. She had a first aid kit in her hand.

"Excuse me, Suzanna," I said. "Sure, David," said Suzanna.

I followed Dalarna back to a room in the complete tail of the plane. We walked through the door, and she asked me to sit on a box. It appeared to be a stockroom of sorts.

"So, Mr. Rutherford, what do you do?" asked Dalarna.

"Call me David," she said.
"I'm an author," I told her.
"Oh really?" said Dalarna.

She took out the alcohol wipes and began to clean the wound.

"Fuck!" I said. It burned like hell!

"Sorry," said Dalarna. "It looks pretty deep. You really need stitches. I think I have some butterfly bandages in here," said Dalarna.

"What are you, a nurse too?" I asked.

"Actually, I'm studying to be one!" she playfully

said.

As she leaned in to apply the stitch bandage, her tits just fell into my face. OK, this just got real! I took the invitation, grabbed her hips, pulling her in. She met my lips as we began to kiss. Of course, I had to take a taste test on those tits. Yep, delicious!

"Oh, Mr. Rutherford, would you like me to help you with that?" she said. She removed her top. No way! What the fuck is up with these Cloudy Sky's girls?? Fuck yea!

Time for talk had passed, it was go-time! I was the driver, and Dalarna was my Ferrari! I took that first aid shit, tossed it aside. I put Dalarna on the counter and took that skirt and panties off with the quickness. She was tugging my hair like she was holding on for dear life as I enjoyed eating that pussy.

We were in quite the time crunch, so she grabbed my belt and whipped it off like Indiana Jones with his whip. Snap, it went! She took my cock and put that fucker right where she wanted it. I dug it as deep as it would go. She tried not to moan, but I was smashing that pussy all too well! Those pussy walls tightened, and there was no holding back! I unleashed a cum to fill her with joy! As I pulled my pants up, she kissed my lips with a shaken embrace.

"Thank you, David," Dalarna said. I kissed her a moment longer, then headed for the restroom. Now I had to take a shit? Fucking Taco Bell!

3. OH SUZANNA

As I sat down, Dalarna was out serving nuts and shooters. Hell fuckin' yeah. "I'll take six of everything... the Lemon Drops!" I told her. As she handed me the nuts, she had written her number down. She was definitely getting a house call... my Swedish nurse!

Dalarna gave my ass a squeeze just as Suzanna looked up! She smiled... Oh, Suzanna, yum! I really need to go to Germany more often.

"So, David, you look satisfied," said Suzanna.
"Yes, as a matter of fact, I am," I said.

"So, David, please tell me where you get your inspiration for your writing?" she asked.

"Well, I would definitely have to show you," I told her.

"Oh my, David, is that an invitation?" said Suzanna. Hmmmm... is it possible to bang two women in one flight? Yep!

"Follow me," she told me as she got up, leaning over, her hand on my cock.

"Oh my, nice package, David," she said. Oh no, no, no, I was not wasting this invitation. NOPE! She took us into the bathroom I had just shit in. Damn! Bad breath, now a shit smell, nooooo! I popped the last 6 mints and thought, fuck it!

As we walked towards the restroom, I noticed a Hitler wannabe with a swastika on his neck. Weird. We got in, and it actually smelled clean? Weird! She stripped down, and there she was—she was in nothing! Love it!! My little German devil.

"I want you to show me that inspiration now!" she said, smiling. I stripped my fucking clothes off immediately! She grabbed my cock and began to bite me? Hell to the fuckin' yeah! I spun her around and grabbed her two braids. I pounded that pussy like the mare she was. Rode her hard and fast. She was loving it, screaming on every thrust like she was on a Six Flags roller coaster on a hot summer day! At the moment that I was about to just explode, I spun her around! She took that cock out of this world!

4. I WAS SHOCKED AND DISAPPOINTED

We were about to land when Suzanna asked for my autograph in her copy of Miss Lacy. It was my first request for one, so it was pretty cool! I wrote:

"Oh Suzanna, My Dearest Fan. I will never forget that flight to L.A. If you are ever in L.A. again, call me xxxxxx-xxxx."

Your Biggest Fan,

David Rutherford

As the plane landed and taxied in, we came to a rest at the gate. What a flight! Much better than the "Tranny's on a Mother Fuckin' Plane!!!" flight.

Suzanna stood up, gave my cheek a peck, and squeezed my cock. Hell to the fuckin' yeah! She took my hand and wrote her number on it.

"Be good, kitten," I told her.

"Ich auf den ersten Blick Schwanz, my dear David," she said as she grabbed my cock.

As I walked out of the plane's corridor, Dalarna was greeting everyone. She kissed me and whispered, "Call me, David" in my ear.

"I definitely will," I told her. Onto baggage claim.

I walked up to baggage claim to pick up my golf clubs. I planned on trying to get in a few rounds while in Vegas with Aila. She was a fuckin' badass when it came to golf!

As I approached the counter, I tried to hand this sorry excuse for a man my claim ticket.

"Step back, sir! Or I will be forced to call security!" he said. "Read the sign!"

"Please Wait Behind the Line"
There was a red-taped line with no one waiting. I mean, this guy smelled of vomit, vodka, and hot dogs?! Yuck! I don't know who pissed in this guy's Wheaties, but I stepped back.

I waited 20 minutes while this FAT fuck shoved raw hot dogs doused in ketchup into his mouth! Every time he finished one, he licked each finger. Gross...

I could only imagine his apartment on a Saturday night. Him and his girl watching porn. The pair tipping the scales over 700 pounds, eating raw hot dogs and Kit Kats?! Washing it down with Dr. Pepper Big Gulps. Oh fuck, I just vomited in my mouth.

Now this was getting ridiculous. 40 minutes had passed, and he was still eating?? "Hey, can I just get my golf clubs? They're right behind you," I asked.

"Sir, I am busy. When I get a moment, I will retrieve your possessions!" said the fat Cheesedick.

My legs were seriously starting to rubberize. I looked at my watch. 25 minutes to catch my flight?!

"Hey, fatty, I have a connecting flight in 25 minutes. Can I get my fucking property?" I said.

"Sir, one more outburst, and I will have to call security with that sort of behavior!" the fat fuck said. He reached down and slapped a name plaque on the counter:

Wayne-Whitmer: Manager on Duty

Who did this guy think he was? Fuckin' cocksucker! The line was 10 deep now. I was giving this guy 5 minutes. I had a screaming baby behind me, the God damn pissed-off, crying Nancy rehearsing his bitch-out speech, and the totally odd couple who lost their drugs and were jonesing to find their lost luggage behind me. I swear, I had enough of this fat fucking, stupid-ass, miserable piece of shit!!

"Look here, Whitmer...! I need my God damn fucking golf clubs NOW!!" I said.

Whitmer's pussy ass picked up the phone, calling security.

—-2 minutes later—-

"Sir, put the bag down and step over here!" security said with tasers drawn.

"Look, I just want my property..." I was saying when...

"Gun!!"

Faded out...

5. TRANNY-CON FUCKS ME

As I opened my eyes, I was handcuffed on a cot in a cell. What the fuck?? My head was splitting, and I needed a fucking scotch! A guy in a blue uniform came to the cell door.

"Mr. Rutherford, you're being booked for disturbing the peace, assaulting a Homeland Security Officer, and attempting to escape," he said.

What the fuck was he saying?! All I wanted was my God damn golf clubs!

"What are you talking about??" I asked.

"Wayne Whitmer is pressing charges, too. There were 9 witnesses, and we'll have you out in 2 to 3 days," he said.

"Oh no, no, no... I have a meeting in less than 24 hours I have to be at!" I said.

"You can bail out. The number is on the wall next to the phone," he said.

He walked out. As I turned to use the phone, there was a guy lying in his own vomit on the floor beneath it. Fuck me! After 32 attempts, I finally got through to the bail bonds company. They wanted a fucking lifetime of information and 60 forms of payment. Fuck me!

They booked me, fingerprinted me, gave me a court date, and finally released me. Now it's 20 hours until my life-changing meeting in Vegas, and I still didn't have my golf clubs!! FML!! Fuck them, I'll buy new ones.

I went to Cloudy Skies to rebook another flight.

"Yeah, I was arrested and missed my flight. Can I have it rebooked?" I asked.

The woman began typing.

"Sir, you didn't elect for the insurance. You'll need to book a new flight," she said.

Insurance? Fuck...

"Ok, at this point, just book me another flight as fast as possible," I asked.

She began typing.
"Soonest possible is the 17th at 10 a.m.," she said.

"What?! I need to be there in 20 hours, not 4 days!" I said.

"Sorry, sir, everything is full to Vegas," she said.

I took my card and ID, shoved them in my wallet, and walked to the other counters. Nothing until the 17th??
What the fucking hell was going on?

A lady behind me said, "It's 'Tranny-Con.' Vegas is full tomorrow."

Are you shitting me? What the fuck was TrannyCon?? I had, had it with fucking trannies! I called Aila.

"Hey Aila, missed my flight due to a hot dog-eating fat fuck. There are no flights until Tuesday! Can you reschedule the meeting?" I asked her.

"Nope," she said.
"Fuck," I replied.

"David, I pulled every string I could to get this sitdown. It's my reputation here. Better get here by 10 a.m. tomorrow."

Click. Phone call ended.

Ok, think, David... Rent a car. Yeah, that's it. I walked to the Thrifty counter. All booked. Enterprise. Booked. Budget. Booked. What the fuck? How big is Tranny-Con?

That left two options: train or Greyhound. Train it is. It was a risk, but it put me in Vegas at 6 a.m. tomorrow. I booked it. Here we go!

6. MNM'S-NUTTY

I had a couple of hours until boarding time for the train. There's this cool bar just down the street from the train station. Time for a quality scotch.

Man, I had a burn the size of a softball on my chest from those fucking tasers. That scotch was just what the doctor ordered.

As I pulled up, it was packed. I was walking in and noticed something really fucking familiar. A shit ton of trannies! Well, I was here, and the Uber driver was gone. I asked the door attendant to leave my bags. He handed me a ticket and pointed me over to the bar after checking my
ID.

I walked up and told the bartender, "A double scotch on ice." As I went to hand him my credit card, in my right ear, I heard, "What's up, my nigga!" she said. I turned into a white, cornrowed, gold-sunglassed, pants-to-hisknees guy wearing a shirt that said, "My Nigga."

"Yes," I said. That was all I could get out. I was speechless. The tranny was just too much. She was slurping on a giant pickle like she was polishing a knob?? I was doing everything possible not to watch, but I couldn't help it. I was stuck.

"My nigga... My nigga... You must be the male entertainment I ordered from Heavy B's?" she said. I still couldn't talk.

Fuck it, I had to play along. "No, sorry, here for the scotch," I said.

"Ok, ok... I bet you can give a hell of a lap dance! MnM's they call me. White chocolate from East Side Rodeo Drive. Head of the Gay Boy Gangstas," said MnM. Ok, I'm trying so hard not to ROFL, but fuck, what a day this was!

"Bartender, this man's tab is on MnM's. My nigga, you sittin' with us," MnM said.

Ok, ok, why not? I was actually just getting used to these folks. We walked over, and there were 3 other trannies at the table.

"This is 'Juggz,' lead singer of the band 'Chicks with Dicks,' headlining Tranny-Con," said MnM.
Juggz shook my hand.

"Nice to meet you," said Juggz.
"Oh, sorry, sorry, I am David Rutherford," I said.
"This is 'Dookie,' lead bassist," said MnM.

I waved; he winked and fluttered his fingers. I couldn't help but think, damn, these trannies have a whole society of their own.

"Last but not least... drum roll please... Tommy D!

He's the fastest tranny drummer on the West Coast!" said MnM.

"Nice to meet you, David," said Tommy. "Likewise," I said.

"Oh my! Pull up next to me, handsome," said Dookie.

"I guess you're heading to Tranny-Con?" I asked while sitting.

"Well, we're trying to get there," said Juggz.

"So, David, are you heading to Tranny-Con too?" asked Dookie.

"No, I'm trying to get to Vegas. Long story... I have a meeting at 10 a.m.," I said.

"Oh, handsome, we have time. Spill the beans," said Dookie.

"Ok, sure, why not? I'm a storyteller for a living," I said.

"Really? You write books then?" asked Juggz.

"Yeah, I'm an author," I said.

"Really? What type of books?" asked Juggz.

"Weird, erotic horror thrillers," I told him.

"Cool. Anything we would know?" asked Dookie.

"Miss Lacy is my most recent," I said. "Cool! I've read it. Love it! The scene with Miss Lacy fucking the guy while she slits his throat, watching him bleed out!" said Dookie.

"Damn, my nigga... You are one fucked-up writer. Cool shit!" said MnM.

"Tell us the story. I can't wait!" said Dookie.

<u>David speaks:</u>

"Well, I can't tell the story in its entirety. It would ruin the book, but... I was going to Berlin, and Russian trannies hijacked the plane. I met Jesse and stayed in Berlin with her. We took the plane back. It was a fucking hell of a flight. Now I'm heading to Las Vegas for a hopeful book signing worth 7 figures," I said.

"I heard about that! One of my boys was on that flight, Stevie. He works for Cloudy Skies," said Tommy D.

"You hooked up with Jesse. We've met her a bunch with Stevie. How's she doing?" asked Dookie.

"Yeah, what a small world," said Tommy D.

"Bartender, bring my niggas another round of Patron, please!" said MnM.

"So, Jesse?? Gotta know if you're still with her," said Dookie.

"Nope," I said, pointing at my butterfly stitches.

"Oh snap! My nigga, she whipped your ass!" said MnM.

"Ooooiii... Single now, huh?" said Dookie.
"Sorry, Dookie, I'm strictly a pussy guy," I said.
"Oh, don't knock it till you try it!" said Dookie.
"Behave," said Juggz.

"Yeah, Jesse used to be into porn. She can't get any new gigs. She keeps fucking up the guys. They'd get too rough on the anal sex scenes. That's what I heard," said Tommy D.

"Yeah, everyone knows to use Astroglide... Duh??" said Dookie.

"True dat... My nigga... That shit's amazing," said MnM.
Ok, this shit was getting a little too deep!

"Porn? Really?? I guess that makes sense," I said.

She really did give a great blowjob, I thought. So I know why now. Plenty of practice. I just didn't realize she had that kind of wear on those tires.

7. BAM-BAM

"My nigga, my nigga Bam-Bam!" said MnM.

"MnM, what's up, you wannabe pop star??" said Bam-Bam.

Now, this was one classy CAT. Where do I start? About 5'2", wearing one of those circus Ringmaster suits wit top hat included! It was the 16-hole laced-up Doc Martens that really set it off. Or maybe it was the big-ass cane with a demon where you grip it? A real character, for sure!

"So, how's Chicks with Dicks doing?" asked BamBam.

"Good, touring as usual. Just finished a big run-in. We got word of the Tranny-Con gig, couldn't turn it down," said Juggz.

"Yeah, lions, tigers, and trannies! Couldn't turn it down either. The offer was too much," said Bam-Bam.

From what I could tell, Bam-Bam was an old gangster. I guess I'll have to keep going to find out more?

"Hey Bam, this is my nigga David Rutherford. This nigga writes BAD ASS, demented, sexual freedom, cool-ass novels!" said MnM.

Now MnM was eating a banana all gay as hell. Really? Licking it and everything! This had to be one of the craziest characters I have ever met. Definitely putting a note upstairs...

But Bam-Bam was something new. Trannies here, trannies there, trannies fucking everywhere!

"How are you, David? Nice to meet you. Are you coming to the shows?" asked Bam-Bam.

"It's been a crazy fucking day. Came for some drinks, so why not the shows?" I said.

"Well, Bam, have a seat. MnM said he's buying the drinks. You gotta catch up; you're two shots behind," said Juggz.

"Another round of Patron!" MnM told the bartender.

"You see, me and Bam served in the Iraq War together. We were explosive experts, and Dookie was our trigger man. We had a nickname for our special forces team: 'The Pink Panthers.' We rained destruction on anyone in our path," said Juggz.

"Snap... my niggas. I never knew that," said MnM.

What was with this guy? MnM had a corn dog now, sliding it in and out of his mouth. This motherfucker was strange as hell.

"Well, to my sistas!" Bam raised his shot glass and downed the first, then the second! We all took our shots.

"Gotta run and catch a train," said Bam-Bam.
"So do we," said Juggz.
"How about you, David?" said Bam.

"Believe it or not, so do I," I said.

"Ok, see you guys on the Tranny Train," said Bam. Ok, what are the chances?

8. BAD IDEA

I headed to the exit to get my bag, and Bam was all upset with the doorman. He was screaming something about his Ric Flair original coat on the floor. He was pissed!

Bam unsheathed a long blade from inside his cane?! Let's just say I grabbed my stuff, and we booked it. What happened next is a true story, I swear! This motherfucker had a midnight blue Bentley limousine! I cannot make this shit up!

"Get in before the cops get here!" said Bam. We jumped in, and the driver sped away. Bam said, "We should hit up the liquor store!" I agreed. We had an hour until the train was scheduled to depart. A couple of drinks couldn't hurt, right?

Well, guess what? BAD IDEA totally! This is what happened. He told the driver to stop at the liquor store.
What happened next was NUTS!

Ok, we've all been to a train or bus station, right? Where do they usually put them? In shitty neighborhoods! What I'm about to tell you is definitely insane! Ok, let's get on with it.

So, our first mistake was that we should have stayed our happy asses in the Bentley! It had a fucking drive-thru! Second, we were in a midnight blue Bentley limousine! What could draw more attention?

As we went into the liquor store, Bam was super fucked up. How did this cat go from intense Ric Flair... Wooooo!...

to a teetering zombie?! Anyway, Bam grabbed a can of Beanie Weenies and started laughing. I told him, "Chill out, Bam. You're going to get us busted!" That totally went in one ear and out the other!

Bam was lit! Whatever he was smoking in the Bentley obviously worked! He was high-stepping in those midnight blue Doc Martens like the floor was on fire. The lava walk with a hint of the spins.

Somehow, Bam managed to make it to the counter with about four boys' worth of stuff. Really? There were three bags of Doritos. All the flavors, six Milky Ways, Skittles, four Slim Jims, and a bag of microwavable popcorn. Seriously, what in the fuck was he going to do with that? The station didn't even have a microwave!

He started the lava walk again. I tried to stop him.
"BAM!"
"Big Gulp, Dr. Pepper."
"Fuck it," I said.

I walked to the counter. There he was, the Middle Eastern Sheik, Akbar.

"You tell friend no steal, I call cops!" he said.

This guy had at least 16 inches of bulletproof glass between us, but he still had a look of terror on his face. I mean, what was so odd here? A tranny in a pearl white, long Ric Flair coat and midnight blue Doc Martens, lacedup boots? Or the lava walk?

Or a long-haired, stoned, drunk, out-of-his-mind white dude in the middle of the hood? Yeah, a little suspect. I turned to tell Bam, "Let's go," and...

"Damn it, Bam!" I said.
"What?" he replied.

I opened his jacket, and at least 32 items fell out. Not including the stuff stuffed in his pants! I grabbed the stuff and threw it on the counter. I looked at Bam.

"What? My wallet's in the car," he said.
"What the fuck?" I said.

I tossed a C-note under Akbar's little stainless slide so he wouldn't have to risk his life trying to collect his American Dream. As I turned, Bam was teetering, slurping that Dr. Pepper, looking at me all weird and shit!

"Let's go, Bam!" I said.

He followed behind me like a scolded dog. I also had to carry all six fucking bags out, then... Our driver was on the ground, unconscious, and... no fucking car!

"You okay?" I asked the driver.

He groaned and rolled over. He had a large gash on his forehead. I turned, and Bam was dancing in circles, singing Celine Dion.

"Bam, get over here!" I said.

So here we were in the hood. No car, fucked-up driver, and no phone. At least I still had the 9mm Bam handed me in the Bentley. Fuck it, we had to make this train!

"Let's try to grab a metro. It's only a little way to the train station," I said.

The driver was up now.
"You okay?" I asked him.

He replied, "Yes." He told us he stepped out to smoke, and two guys pistol-whipped him and stole the car.
Fuck!

We stumbled to the bus stop, and a couple of homeless folks were camped out. I had to bribe them with the rest of my cash and half of Bam's groceries to move on!

"Sit down, Bam!" I said.

He was acting like he was having an EPI! I mean, fuck, what did he smoke in the Bentley?? The bus pulled up, and the driver and Bam stumbled in. Of course, I had to pay. Fuck, I was out of cash! The bus driver pointed at the digital pay pad. I pulled out my credit card, which was almost maxed out!

9. THE NAZIS

I went to sit down.

"Give me a bottle and a Honey Bun," Bam said.

"You fucking kidding me, Drama Queen?" I said.

I threw him the tequila and a Honey Bun. We said, "Fuck it," and drank the tequila before heading to the train station. Bam also devoured four Honey Buns.

We hurried to check in, just barely making it! The attendant told me, "Seat 21?" Really, this is turning into a broken record. This whole situation was seriously giving me a severe migraine!

As I looked out into the crowd, I noticed six savory figures. Déjà vu! Instead of fucking trannies, these were a different breed—Nazis?! How lucky can a guy be, seriously? Bam disappeared as I went to sit. It was none other than... yes... oh my Suzanna! What the fuck was she doing here? Well, I knew one part of my body that was extremely happy!

"What's up, kitten?!" I said.

"David!!!"

She hopped up, hugging me like one of those cute koala bears!

"How the fuck did this happen, my beautiful German princess?!" I said.

"I don't know, but I am so happy!"

She was kissing my neck and nibbling my ear. Oh no, I had better stop this before we both end up naked! She hopped down.

"So, what should we do with ourselves until Vegas, doll?" I asked.

"Hmmm... I have a few ideas, David," she said playfully.

Oh fuck, those Honey Buns, Slim Jims, and tequila were calling out very loudly!

"I'll be back, love," I told her.

"Okay, David," she said, as she began reading Miss Lacy.

Man, I had to hurry. This turtle head was as wild as one of those enormous sea turtles, fins and all! I needed to book it!

As I was scooting... You know the scoot? I know you do! The one where your left hand is on your ass cheeks and your right hand is waving like an essay? Yeah, you know it.

I was scooting and noticed that the neck-swastika Nazi guy from the plane was here as well. This is way too coincidental! He was sitting next to another Nazi fuck, with "Fuck Off" tattooed across his forehead! Real fucking creepy. Ten feet to the restroom... fuck, I'm going to shart myself... six feet... three feet... I literally kicked the door in! I dove into the stall!

SPLAT! Oh fuck, yeah! Now I had cat breath and a shit stain?! FML!

I finished shitting and decided to take a sink bath. I needed some new shorts pretty badly; maybe one of the trannies had some extra boxers?

I headed back to my Suzanna, and the Nazi fuck grabbed my arms all aggressively!

"Be a good boy, Mr. Rutherford. Suzanna is a very important person," he said.

I shrugged him off and gave him the landscaper stare. As I walked, I could feel that Nazi stare burning a hole in me. Creepy!

As I sat down, Suzanna asked, "What's wrong, David?"
"Nothing, I had a stomach cramp," I told her.

"Oh," she replied.

Yeah, probably not sexy talk, but at the moment, it was all I had. As we sat in silence, the train's brakes squealed and it began to move.

I was lost in thought about all of this. My jaw was killing me. She kept reading, and I stayed lost in my head.

10. FAMILY AFFAIRS

As the train began to pick up speed outside the city, folks started to move about. I couldn't help but think something bigger was brewing on this train to Las Vegas!

My gut told me it was no good as well.

I told Suzanna, "Fuck it, let's go get a drink," and she was down. So, we walked through the cars. She knew exactly where to go. I found that kind of odd. What was this all about? I had that same spidey sense I had on the plane.

As we went through the kitchen to get to the bar dining car, the staff were all speaking German to Suzanna.

Weird again. Who the fuck was my fuck toy? We walked in and, yep... a full car of drunk...

"Mother fucking tranny's on a train!"

Yes, there was the full circus crew and Juggz and his crew, but the guys who really stood out were the six crazy-ass looking white boys at the table in the back.

Suzanna ran across the room, heading straight to them.

"Daddy!" said Suzanna.

Okay, what the fuck was going on? Daddy? Mr. Fuck Off was her father?! Okay, I had to go over now and meet Mr. Fuck Off.

"Let's sit down with my father and his associates, David!" said Suzanna.

"Okay," I said.

There was one chair, so I wasn't exactly sure what the plan was here. She continued blinking at me as if I knew. Fuck it, I sat down, and she hopped into my lap.

Awkward moment.

"Daddy, David will take a double scotch on the rocks, right David?" she said.

"Yes, that would be nice, Suzanna," I said.

She was playing with my cock, and these dudes were definitely noticing.

"I'll take a Tequila Sunrise," she said.

"Okay, Suzy. So it's David? What is it you do, David?" asked her father.

"Oh, he writes books! He's a famous author!" she said.

"Famous author, Mr. David? Sorry, I did not catch your last name," he asked.

"Not famous, sir. I am a struggling author, trying to make it. David Rutherford is my full name, sir," I said.

"Charles Cross," he said.

He reached across the table, sporting a swastika on his hand. I shook his hand as he death-gripped mine.

"Nice to meet you," I told him.

"This is Hans, Chuck, Franz, Tony, and Victor," he said.

"Nice to meet all of you," I said.

They all nodded. Swastika neck gave me the side eye. I felt like this crowd was seriously deciding which torture tools to use on me. Not a smile at the table besides Suzanna.

"Daddy, David is on his way to Vegas to meet a big publishing company to sign a major book deal!" said Suzanna.

"That's impressive, David. I look forward to hearing more about this another time. We have business to deal with, Suzy. You can hang out at the bar. Thomas will serve your friends, on me," said Charles.

"Okay, Daddy, thank you!" she said.

As the crew stared at me, shooting bullets into my skull, I got Suzanna up and told them, "Thank you," and turned with Suzanna, holding my hand to the bar. I felt like a teenager meeting parents, getting permission to court her.

It reminded me of a story I just have to tell her someday, but today we had bigger fish to fry. These were no normal Captain D's fillets! Oh no, straight-up catfish, wharf shit, the big-ass, nasty fillets!

This was a weird family affair.

11. FUCK ME... FUCK ME TWICE

Okay, first Russian tranny terrorists? Now, crazy, insane Nazis? I know Chuck had to be an Alabama-style KKK racist. He was wearing coveralls, for fuck's sake! Hans was a full-blown, sandy blonde, stereotypical wannabe Adolf. Tony had to be an Italian racist. I know, weird as hell!

"Fuck me... Fuck me twice!"

Really? Instead of greed and lust, it's hate and disgust? Only one way out of this one.

"Mother fucking trannies on a train!"

Thomas approached. I heard over my shoulder...

"My nigga! Mr. David Rutherford!" said MnMs.

Oh fuck, this was going to be interesting for sure! Suzanna was going to freak on these chicks! Okay, did I just seriously think that?

"And who is this hot baby mama?" MnMs said.

"Suzanna Andstrom, and who is this hot playgirl?" said Suzanna, chuckling.

"Oh shit, nigga, I like this one... Sassy baby mama for sure!" said MnMs.

"This is MnMs, a rap artist for Tranny-Con," I said.

"Tranny-Con? Oh, please explain!" said Suzanna.

"Well, girl, it's a tranny extravaganza! All the new hormone meds! The new app-operated fuck toys and coolas-hell doctors for sure! A full circus, my rap show, and live metal! Celebrities signing autographs! Last but not least, all my homies!" said MnMs.

About that time, Bam rolled up on our front porch. He was sporting his pimp attire. Where did he get new shit? They stole the Bentley?

"Davey-Boy," said Bam.

"Hey, Bam," I said.

"Who the fuck is this? She's hot! Girl, who does your hair?" said Dookie.

Oh shit, Dookie too?

"It's a woman in Berlin. She's amazing! She does the best Brazilian Blow I have ever had!" said Suzanna.

"Oh, you have never seen my Brazilian Blow girl!" said Dookie.

"Dookie, respect David's friend," said Juggz as he sat down.

"My nigga Juggz! This princess is treating us to Tequila Sunrises!" said MnMs.

"Well, what's your name, princess? Please tell me it's not Leia," said Juggz.

Well, she was sporting the two Princess Leia hair buns! It was really sexy too! I always wanted to bang her for real!

"Suzanna Andstrom, the future Mrs. Rutherford!" said MnMs.

"Wow, hold on there, White Chocolate!" I said.

Suzanna gave me the drunken eyebrow. Thank God the tequila bottles were behind the bar.

"What, am I not pretty enough for you, DaveyBoy?" said Suzanna.

"Oooooooohweee," said Dookie.
"Ha... Ha..." I told Dookie.
"Well???" said Suzanna.

"Okay, I'm not saying that. I am just saying... Fuck it, let's move on with this! You fuckers quit! Suzanna and I are friends, fuck you, Dookie!" I said.

"Oh really, and that's why you're not getting fucked!" said Suzanna.

"Ummmmm... Okay??" I said.

As I turned, Suzanna was across the room with Dookie. Bam was having an EPI. Juggz and Tommy D were in one of those deep conversations. I took this as a cue to get cleaned up.

"Hey Bam, I need those clothes, man. Where is your luggage?" I asked.

"Mmmmmtsst wark," said Bam.

"He's in seat 116, above it. The rest is in the luggage car, probably," said Juggz.

"Thanks," I said.
As I looked around, the Nazi table was now empty.

As I weaved my way through the car to 116 to get some fresh duds, hopefully to save face with Suzanna, I passed a large room. Inside of it were some Nazis with Charles Cross. Completely new guys? What was going on here? It smelled a lot like the plane.

As I opened Bam's overhead, a ton of shit fell out. This guy was a five-foot-two-inch slob! For real? As I started to pick it up, there were blueprints to Circus and German receipts for plutonium. Crazy shit. Oh shit!

"Fuck me... Fuck me twice."

12. A REAL COCKSUCKER

Okay, what were these Nazis up to? What or why did Bam have to do with it? I picked everything up, including the glass crack pipe. I grabbed the soaps, lotion, and fresh clothes. I had to find Juggz. Our only chance to stop this terrorism plot!

As I walked to the restroom, I couldn't help but think what a cocksucker, for real! A real cocksucker in every sense! Also, was Suzanna a part of it? I really couldn't see that. I had to go encyclopedia brown and investigate!

As I was cleaning up...

"My nigga, your girl was looking for you!" said MnMs.

"Really, how come?" I asked.

"She asked me to pimp her up! I put some tight clothes on her. Dookie is with her doing makeup. She likes you, nigga, pretty good!" said MnMs.

This was an awkward moment for sure. I needed to change, and he was just watching all weird with a lollipop all weird and shit.

"Hey, gotta change, MnMs," I said.
"And?" said MnMs.
"Privacy maybe?" I replied.
"Oh, nigga, chill," he said.

I decided to just step into the stall. It wasn't very big, so this was a challenge.

"So, what do you think of Suzanna's dad and the white dudes?" I asked.

"They seem too legit to quit, for sure!" he said.
"MnMs, I need a favor," I said.
"For sure, G," he said.

"Are you heading back to hang out with Suzanna?" I asked.

"Yeah, I need to drop a deuce first, though," he said.

"Ummmmmm... Okay, never heard that before. Can you pick at her to find out about her father's family?
Why are they going to Vegas?" I said.

"Ain't no thang but a chicken wang, G! I'll be your dick-tective!" said MnMs.

I had no response. He was standing there, licking Cheetos and shit. Where did he get all this food? Why did he eat it all weird? Only MnMs. He was a strange cat for sure.

"Sounds good. Keep her busy a bit, okay? I have some business to attend to," I said.

"Check ya! I get what you're dealing with for sure. You got a side hustle on, baby mama! Don't worry, my nigga, your secrets are safe with this nigga! Thug life! Gotta pay the rent!" he said.

"Yeah," I said.

MnMs dipped into the shitter, and I threw my nasty clothes into the waste can.

"Meet me at the bar in an hour, okay?" I asked.

"Okay, my nigga!" said MnMs.

13. OPERATION NAZI-ZAPPER...BUZZ

I headed to the bar to find Juggz. I had a serious feeling starting for Suzanna. She was beautiful, funny, and innocent... all the qualities I would marry. The problem was, she was a co-conspirator in mass murder. Yeah, that would be a deal breaker. My luck too. What is it with me and women?

I did know one thing for sure: Bam was a backstabbing piece of shit. He was obviously involved with these Nazis. Probably in some way, a drug debt. Probably an 805 bitch. He was not only trying to blow up my friends but half of Vegas! My friends? Well, my life was definitely different for sure.

Yeah, they were my friends. Suzanna had a chance of being a serious one. I was struggling a lot these last few months.

I walked up to the bar, and it was getting close to 11:30. We had less than eight and a half hours to stop a massive nuclear explosion, have a romantic evening, and save...

"Mother fuckin' Tranny's on a Train!"

No Juggz, just Judaist himself. He was still stumbling around with butthole EPI face.

"Bam, where are Juggz and Tommy D?" I asked.

He just gave me the landscaper stare, blinking. "Lett kiark filft money?" said Bam.

"You need to sober up, dude, really?" I said.

I told Thomas to cut him off. I had shit to deal with. Thomas told me Juggz and Tommy D were watching a movie in the cinema car. I thanked him and felt like slapping that little Carney fuck, Bam!

We had to find Juggz, make a plan, and stop this train from vaporizing us in the desert. No biggie. All I could think was…

"Where's the Beef?"
Just kidding, that's Wendy's. I know. Try again.
"Mother Fucking Tranny's on a Train!"
As I approached…

"Juggz, can you and Tommy come out to the corridor?" I asked.

"What? Jason vs. Freddy just started," said Tommy.

"It's important!" I said.
"Okay," they said.
We stepped into the corridor. "What's up, David?" they asked.

"I need to tell you about some heavy shit. It has to be kept undercover till we find out the details," I said.

"Okay, David," they said.

"Okay, I was going through Bam's stuff when I found some blueprints to Circus and some German receipts for plutonium. I think he wants to blow up Tranny-Con in Vegas," I told them.

They sat there with a landscaper stare, then Juggz said...

"Tommy, get our weapons and ammo together. I and David will see what we can find out about the bombs. Also, we will need Dookie for the triggers, Oso for the heavy lifting, and Cruz to run decoy on the Nazis," said Juggz.

"Sounds good. I will get them together. Here's a 40 and a couple clips. Call me," said Tommy.

"Hey, Dookie is with MnMs and Suzanna right now," I blurted out.

"What the fuck?" said Juggz.
"Is she part of it?" asked Tommy.

"I don't know yet," I replied.
"Ten-four. I will handle it," said Tommy.

We split up, and Juggz and I started our way to the tail of the train where luggage was located. Juggz said it was the only good place to store a bomb of that size. It was time for Operation Nazi-Zapper to start for the...

"Mother Fuckin' Tranny's on a Train!"

14. JOHNNIE (JUGGZ) JONES

As we were walking car to car, I asked Juggz to tell me more about the military background of the guys. He began to tell me...

<u>Juggz Talking</u>

"It was 2001, and we were ordered into the heart of the enemy. It was a special squad of 'Don't ask, Don't tell.' We were all Special Forces, but no one but our commanding officer knew our mission. We banded together, forming the 'Pink Panthers.' Our specialty was explosives. This particular mission was to infiltrate into Baghdad and shove a lot of C-4 up Saddam Hussein's ass! Well, Sergeant Major Tommy Masorte was our sniper.

Willie 'Dookie' Johnson, 1st Sergeant, was our trigger man and explosives expert. Sergeant Oso was our heavy lifter. Expert in heavy caliber artillery, and Lieutenant was a linguist and wheelman. He was always trying to make a deal somewhere or score pussy somehow. He was a hell of a talker in seven languages and a primo wheelman. Sergeant was a bear when it came to bulldozing shit! A wrecking ball! Sergeant Major Tommy Masorte could hit a dime half a mile away. 1st Sergeant Willie Johnson held a record of destroying a brigade sequentially without a bullet fired. So David, this train is in good hands. Only Rambo could be better!" said Juggz.

"Well then, let's fuck up some Nazis," I said.

"Let's find the explosives first, Private Rutherford," said Juggz.

We were about a car away from the luggage car when Juggz shoved me into the restroom.

"Be quiet," he said.

The door closed, a minute or so passed, then Thud...Arghh...The door opened, and Juggz dragged a dead Nazi in and set him on the toilet.

"They have sentries everywhere. Means we are close," said Juggz.

"Okay," I said.
"Do I get a gun?" I asked.
"Here," Juggz said.

He handed me the pistol and whipped out a knife from his 16-hole boots. I was in way over my head.

"Wait here," said Juggz.

He disappeared. I was standing there with a dead man sitting on a toilet looking at me. I did have to take a shit for real. I was not sure how long Juggz would be, but that turtlehead was screaming to be set free! Tequila always makes me want to shit. It reminded me of a story...

I was at a club in Little Rock, Arkansas, with a friend. We discovered a dance club. We were broke as hell, and we went anyway. I could usually talk chicks into buying drinks. It usually came at a price, if you know what I mean. So many nights waking up to a girl I totally don't remember meeting.

Well, that night was girls' night out with Tequila drinks! Half price for the ladies. This was the night I discovered a barking pussy. Yes, barking. I had all my drinks for free, but the price came. We ended up at her apartment and had a few more drinks until...

She got frisky, and after a night of tequila, topping it off with vodka, my mind was a horrible tornado. She actually started to look cute. Well, we ended up in bed, and while I was fucking her...bark...bark, swear to God. I didn't know whether to start laughing or go harder. Yeah, I went harder. She was digging it too.

I woke up the next morning, and she was not cute... Nope. She grabbed my cock through, and I said fuck it and went again.

The moral of the story is that all that tequila and barking made me have to shit. I went to shit, and this broad seriously gave me a blow job while shitting. I gotta admit it was pretty cool, in a weird way. Well, now I had experienced barking pussy and a blow job while shitting.

Now, every time I drink tequila, it makes me want to shit!

15. ALLIED TRANNY FORCES

Well, as I was wiping my ass, chuckling, the door slung open. "David...Yea...Let's go..." It was Juggz.

"I found the bombs. This is pretty bad, David. Remote detonators," said Juggz.

"Okay, and the good news?" I asked.

"I hope we can pull a rabbit out of your ass," said Juggz.

Damn, we had just left the set of *Bullet Train* and stepped into the set of *Broken Arrow*. The good news was we had the "Pink Panthers" on board! Or should I say...

"Mother fuckin Tranny's on a Train!"

Well, if this was going to go south, I really needed Suzanna right now. I mean, fuck, if you're going to be smashed out, then one last ride on the Suzanna Andstrom express is what I needed!

Juggz told me to hurry; we had to meet the crew at the bar.

"What about the dead guy?" I asked.

Juggz grabbed the paper by the sink, put it over the guy's face, and shut the stall. "Let's go!" Juggz said. We took off for the bar to evaluate options, I guess?

Oh fuck me running. There she was... The most attractive woman to date! Beautiful eyes, titties not too big, you know? Saggy titties suck. Well, they can still be sucked on. Never mind. A tight belly, the kind that looks delightful enough to... Her titties were the kind that are more than a handful but small enough not to sag. Just the right amount to squeeze. Like those stress balls. An ass that has enough to jiggle but no cottage cheese. Yuck! A personality that radiates innocence and playfulness at the same time. Oh Suzanna, yes, she was a delight.

"David!" she ran and yelled.

I caught her midair. Oh shit! She was even more stunning with her tranny makeover!

"Hey sexy! I see someone got into someone's beauty bag! You look ravishing!" I said.

"Thank you, David! I did not know if you would notice," she said, nibbling on my ear!

I looked over, and Dookie was already on the move towards the luggage car.

"Hey baby, I need to talk to Juggz and the crew."

I nodded at MnMs, and he grabbed her to the bar for shooters.

"Okay, what can I do, Juggz?" I asked.

"We need you to talk to Suzanna and get her to help you get to the engine so we can take back the train. Alex, our friend at the CIA, did some investigating. Cross Holdings owns multiple aeronautical companies that are government contracted. He has access to everything. He also owns this train. We need you to infiltrate and gain control of the engine with Suzanna's help. It's up to you to convince her. Hopefully, she's not part of their plot. If she is, give her this..." said Juggz.

He handed me a pill.

"It's a tranquilizer to put her to sleep. Tommy will have your six! Here's a radio; put it in your ear. Wait for my signal if we need to blow the engine. In this backpack, after turning the key, we cannot let this train make it to Vegas," said Juggz.

Oh shit, this was real. We were either going to be evaporated or an ex-soldier named Dookie was going to disarm them? The good thing was we were still in the desert. Why does this shit keep happening to me? I swear, on my way back to L.A.... if I survive this...I'm renting a car.

What could go wrong there? Or maybe a boat?

16. FUCK THE CABOOSE – FULL STEAM A-HEAD

Okay, now to tell Suzanna. Last time I sat down with a lady to have a heart-to-heart, I ended up with a tequila bottle to the chin! Here it goes. I walked up to the bar.

"What's up, my nigga!" said MnMs.

"I need to talk to Suzanna," I said, all serious and shit.

"Okay, okay. Chill, Davey Boy... Ice, ice baby. She was just cock-talkin' with M.G. I smell what you're laying down! Try these nuts, extra salty!" said MnMs.

He handed me a bowl of peanuts he was all sucking on. What was with this cat?

"Thanks, MnMs," I said.
"See you soon, MnMs," Suzanna said.
"You too, baby girl!" said MnMs.

It was go time. I had two outcomes here: Suzanna and I take the train back, or I put her to sleep.

"Hey, Suzanna..." I said.
I said it all pussy-like, like I was in preschool!
"Yes?" she said.

"Hold on a sec... Bartender, can we get her another

drink? I'll take a Corona, salt, and lime, please," I said.

She looked very confused about the whole matter. The bartender brought the drinks, and I held the vial of tranquilizer just in case.

"Suzanna, your father plans on nuking Vegas. Bam's part of it, in some scumbag, zombie kind of way. I need to know if you are," I said.

I figured the best way to get to the truth was to just rip the band-aid off quickly!

"Wow!! David, that's a lot... Of course not. How do you know this?" she asked.

"I have proof. A ton of it," I said.

"I need to ask him; this cannot be true. I mean, he has a lot of anger towards Americans. My grandmother was murdered by an American soldier in the war, which he has been avenging. Cold-blooded mass murder? My father is a good man, I promise, David," Suzanna said.

Well, that's hard to believe. A man with a swastika on his hand is a good man! His daughter is sweet, so something in him must be good. Sometimes we start into something that sweeps us into the deep end of the pool before we know how to swim. Then life begins to drown all the life out of us.

"No, you cannot talk to him. We have to stop this train. It has two nuclear bombs in the luggage car," I said, with a pause.

"We saw them with our own eyes," I continued.

Well, she did not try to hit me. That's a good sign. She just sat there, dazed and drinking. It seemed an eternity before she spoke.

"I will help you," she said.

"Okay, let's get you into something more comfortable... wink... wink," I said.

"Oh, David," she said.

"Let's talk more later on that commitment subject. I have room at my condo for two," I said.

"Yummy!" she said.

Even though we barely knew each other, it was a weird attraction, like we had known each other all our lives! She seemed to feel that way also.

We headed to our seats to see about those clothes. As we were walking, it hit me.

"Did you see Bam?" I said.
"Ummmm, no? Not for a while," she said.

Where was that little fucker? What was he up to? That motherfucker was probably dry snitching on us. What a weasel.

As she grabbed her clothes, we went to the ladies' room.

"David, there is something you should know about my family and me," said Suzanna.

17. THE ANDSTROM FAMILY

Okay, here we go! The real truth! I still had that tranquilizer in case this went south.

Suzanna Speaks

"David, my family was deeply rooted in the Nazi Regime. My grandfather worked directly for Joseph Goebbels. He was part of a secret organization that consisted of only a few men. So discreet, even Hitler had no idea. Their vision was to cleanse the world of the impure. My father has fought the organization at the cost of my mother. Since she died, my father has trained me in every lethal technique. I have to be honest, David, I feel really close to you... David, 'I love you.' I know my father would never do this. Do you trust me?" she asked.

"Yes, Kitten, I do," I said.
"Then you have to let me speak to him," she said.
"Okay, Kitten, we will try it your way," I said.
"Thank you, David!" she said.

I mean, fuck it. Having an inside ally could really help the cause here! Plus, there was something about his handshake that made me believe he was a good person inside. Weird, I know.

"I love you, David! I am sure of it! My panties are super wet right now... wink...!" she said.

"This is for your father if he won't help," I said.

I handed her the tranquilizer, and she handed me the key card to access any door on the train.

"Thank you, David. He's my daddy still!" she said.

I grabbed her tight and gave her a Casablanca kiss! She grabbed my cock and said, "Later, baby!"

18. GONNA CATCH ME RIDIN' DIRTY

Here we go again. Sulu, take us out! Yep, I said it! I know Star Wars fans will boycott me, but I love Star Trek too!

"Get your ass moving, Private!" said Tommy over the earpiece.

"Where the fuck are you?" I said.
"Get to the engine, Rutherford!" said Juggz.
"I am working on it," I said.

Damn, now I'm being ordered like a soldier. Well, this is not an episode of *Charles in Charge*, at least. I started moving toward the front of the train.

I made it two cars when... fucking Nazis, no way around?

"Go to the Access Panel Room, 20 meters, then right," said Tommy.

"Okay, now what?" I said.

No response. Man, I felt totally alone here! The door was locked. Oh yeah... Access card... swipe... bleep... green light... click. Hell yeah, I love that woman too!

There were a lot of breakers and switches. I tried Tommy again.

"Fucking Tommy, now what?" I said.

"Hold on, Privates... ha, ha," said Tommy.

"Flip breaker 24, 28, 30 on panel LP-2 when I tell you," he continued.

"Won't that tip them off?" I asked.

"Just do it, David," Tommy said.

"Now," he demanded.

I flipped them. I heard a lot of silencer shots, then quiet... there was a knock.

"Umm, hello?" I said.

"It's Tommy," he said.

I opened the door...

Tommy threw his rifle over his shoulder. He went to the ladder and started climbing to a hatch.

"Go ahead and proceed," said Tommy.

I stepped out, and there were bodies everywhere! Damn, Tommy was a badass motherfucker... or as they say in England... a HARD CASE THUG! I kept going. I saw Suzanna with her father. They were talking, then he rushed down the corridor. Swipe... Nzzz... Red light... Fuck! It did not work on the engine car.

"We have the bombs, Dookie is trying to disarm them," said Juggz.

"We have to stop this train, David, or decouple the part with the bombs," said Tommy.

"I know..." I said.

"David, you're going to have to go up top to get to the engine controls. I will stay at the hatch to provide support until Juggz gets here to blow the door," said Tommy.

Well, fuck, I always said I would never join the military. Yet here we are! I climbed into the hatch and poof, outside the train! Okay, can you say, fucking fast as hell? This motherfucker had to be going over 100 miles per hour! I put the pistol in my waistband.

Fuck it, here we go! I crawled slowly to get to the engine controls car. As I was crawling, I couldn't help but think why they were sending an inexperienced author to operate controls that he had no idea how to operate. Option B was to plant C-4, which I have never done! I don't even know what it looks like. While Seal Team Six is on the other side of the train.

Hmm... yep, I was fucking bait. Not even the good bait. I was the easiest expendable bait. I thought these Trannys liked me. Fucking assholes!

"Tommy, I'm bait, aren't I?" I asked.

I could hardly hang on at 100+ miles per hour. This is no joke! Oh shit, there are a shit ton of Nazis.

All of a sudden, there were flashes everywhere, guys were shooting at me. What the fuck?!

"Fire back," said Tommy.

I fired until the gun flew out of my hand. Then I heard the shotgun, followed by silence... The hatch popped open. Oh fuck... It was Tommy! Fuck yeah. I made it! At least they didn't!

"Catch me ridin' dirty!"

19. OKAY, WHAT YOU'RE SAYING IS I GOTTA CHANCE

Well, I was never so happy to see a tranny! Nor to be off the top of a 100+ mph train. Yes, I said that in the same paragraph! Oh yeah, I gotta say I've spent my whole life not killing anyone, but since my tranny encounter, 5 dead bodies! So much for breaking a guy in slowly. I totally know how Bruce Willis felt in the *Die Hard* series... for real.

As I climbed down, Tommy, Juggz, and all the crew were here! They were all looking at me really weirdly, though.

"Hey... what's up, I think," I said.

"Well, David, the door is magnetically sealed all tight. If we blow it, the engine will separate, and everyone will surely die," said Juggz.

"Okay... So why is everyone looking at me?" I said.

Tommy D lifted a trap door. As I looked down, my life flashed before my eyes, or it might have been the tracks below.

"And who's going down there?" I asked.
"You," said Tommy D.
"Whoa... whoa... whoa," I said.

"You are the only one who can pull this off, Rutherford," said Juggz.

"What about that guy?" I said.

"David, we all need you," said Tommy D. "So what you're saying is I've got a chance?"

"Yeah, it has to be unlocked from the other side manually," said Juggz.

"Oh, fuck it," I said.

Did I seriously just agree to climb under a 100+ mph train to open a magnetically sealed door like in *Snowpiercer*? Oh my God! I really need a shrink after this.

The PTSD alone is going to last for weeks.

"Okay, what about the bombs?" I asked.
"One problem at a time, Rutherford," said Juggz.

As I climbed under, it was nothing like the movies. It actually was not that bad until I got to the junction between the cars.

I had to really stretch to span the gap between the cars. It was a 3-4 foot gap. You know the saying, "stand in the gap" for someone? It had a whole new meaning.

As I stretched, something on the train exploded. I lost my grip and was hanging on by my legs. I could feel the ground below whizzing past. I waited for the nuclear flash, but nothing.

"We uncoupled one car with C-4; its thermonuclear weapon is disarmed," said Dookie.

"The other one is remote detonation only. I am trying to disarm it," Dookie continued.

Nice of him to warn me, I went swinging up like on the preschool monkey bars. 1... 2... 3... swing! Made it! I got to the hatch. I got inside and manually cranked the door.

"Good job, Rutherford!" said Juggz.

"Well, let's get control of this locomotive!" said Tommy D.

20. MEXICAN-TRANNY STANDOFF

Once inside, we had control of the train, but there was another room. Juggz moved to the door and motioned for Tommy D. I just stood there like a dumbass. I had no clue what to do.

Juggz kicked the door after whipping out a shotgun from a pouch and blowing the lock!

It was like Arnold in *Terminator*! Inside was that fuck-face scumbag, Bam! He had Suzanna in an armlock with the remote detonator in his hand.

"If I click this switch, it starts the timer!" said Bam.

At that very second, a shot rang out... Bam fell, and Suzanna ran into my arms! Juggz put the shotgun to Bam's head! Too late...

"Johnnie, timer just started!" said Dookie.
"How long?" said Juggz.
"10 minutes," said Dookie.
"Can you disarm it?" asked Juggz.

"No... I can delay it so we can decouple the train. I need the passcode, though. We can buy enough time to clear the blast," said Dookie.

Juggz looked at Bam.
"I will never tell you," said Bam.

Tommy D whipped out a huge dildo with razor blades laced into it! I did not want to know.

"Is that a Pink Panther special torture device?" I said.

"You two head back to the bar. Keep low-key so as not to create a panic," said Juggz.

"We will take care of Bam and the passcode," said Tommy.

As we walked down the corridor, we could hear Bam squealing like a pig. Man, I have seen some fucked-up shit, but that was by far the most fucked-up shit!

"What happened with your father?" I asked.

"Bam jumped us and shot him. David, can I see him one more time before we die?" said Suzanna.

"Yeah..."

As we got to where Charles Cross was supposed to be, he was not there. What was going on?

"David, you copy?" said Juggz.
"Yeah..." I said.

"Dookie is delaying the timer. Bam gave up the passcode after he got it in the ass! We need to decouple the end of the train. Head to help Dookie move passengers forward," said Juggz.

"Okay," I said.

Suzanna was crying and extremely upset...

"Where is my father? I saw him shot! He was trying to stop the bombs. I told you he was not evil!" she said, sobbing.

"I don't know what is going on, Suzanna. Right now, we have to save the lives on the train and the city of Vegas," I said.

At that moment, Dookie radioed, "The passengers have been moved forward. There is a problem, though... Someone has to manually decouple the cars. They will be left in the blast," said Dookie.

Well, fuck! Every good story always needs a sacrifice, why not? I had to do something.

"Meet at the bar, I have an idea," I said.

"Ten-Four," said everyone.

We got to the bar, and all the passengers looked terrified...

"Suzanna, can you help calm the passengers?" I said.

She looked at me all crazy.

"What the fuck do I look like, a shrink?! I need a fucking martini!" she said.

"Okay then... Thomas, can I get 8 straws, please?" I

said.

I took the straws, cut them into different lengths with scissors, and everyone knew what was happening. We have all seen *Armageddon*.

Fuck me... mine was the shortest. Everyone just stood there.

"I will do it," said Juggz.
"No, I will," said Dookie.
"No! Stop! It was my straw!" I said.
"David..."
Suzanna ran off sobbing...
"Alright, what do I do?" I asked.

"You will need to go below that hatch again and place this C-4 at the coupler. Then take this pin, plug it in, then climb into the car and press this button," said Dookie.

"Once it blows, there is a release lever that must be pulled. Then it will be done. Do not release it, or it will not decouple!" he continued.

"Okay," I said.
About that time, our earpieces...
"Can I talk to Suzy?" Charles Cross said.
I walked to Suzanna...
"It's your father," I said.

Juggz handed me his earpiece to give her.

"Daddy," she said.

"Suzy, I love you. I have to do this. It's my burden to bear, Suzy," Charles Cross continued.

"No, Daddy!" Suzanna said, sobbing.

At that moment, the train shook! Dookie told Oso to put the train at full speed. Juggz told the passengers to prepare for the blast. Dookie said there was 1 minute till the blast and to say goodbye. The radio would lose signal in seconds.

"Daddy, I love you!" she said.

"Suzy, I wish I could have been a better father. Been there to watch you grow and have my grandchild. David, you take care of my little girl. Suzy, I love you more..." Charles Cross said.

The radio lost signal. It was time to brace and hope we were far enough from the blast. Suzanna fell into my arms.

21. FUCKIN OPPENHEIMER

We braced for the thermonuclear explosion. This was totally a scene from *Broken Arrow*, a desert detonation!

"I do love you, Suzanna," I said.
"I love you too, David!" she said.

"If we survive this, do you want to get married?" I said.

"Yes... David, yes!" she said.

Dookie yelled, "30 seconds... 25 seconds... 20 seconds..."

Okay, I am not going to lie; my palms were sweating. I was terrified! Not every day you're in the radius of a thermonuclear bomb!

10... 9... 8... 7... 6... 5... 4... 3... 2... 1

The sky lit up like it was a sunny day at the beach! Everyone gasped. I took a second, and then the train shook... Then it was over! We had survived!

As I looked out the window, you could see the mushroom cloud. For some weird reason, it was beautiful even though you knew its destructive power.

We limped the bullet hole-filled, nuclear-blasted, C-4-jacked train into Las Vegas. It seemed fitting, almost like a scene from its own movie. If it had hubcaps, they would have fallen off when we stopped. And it was on time, believe it or not! I guess that's one thing Cross Holdings could be proud of!

As we arrived, the Circus train pulled in too! All the lions, tigers, and bears, oh my!

I had to make my meeting! After all this, it was my only hope of not being a homeless character in *Scoot Against the World*. I looked over, and Suzanna looked rough. Makeup and mascara were dripping from her sobbing. My phone fell off the train when I was hanging like a monkey from it. So I asked to borrow hers.

Shit, what was Aila's number? I had no ride! I looked up a ride with Uber; it was 2+ hours. Damn, Tranny-Con was a big event. Well, Heel-Toe-Express was the only option, I guess.

"I have an idea!" said Tommy D.

He ran off. Simon and Schuster was over 4 miles from the station, and it was bumper to bumper out front!
Damn!

I kissed Suzanna, told her I would see her at Tranny-Con. It was a long, multiple titty grab, kiss too...
Yummy! As I was about to fire up the Nikes, I heard...

"My nigga! Hold on G! I got something for sure you need!" said MnMs.

MnMs and Tommy D had a zebra?! Oh hell yeah, I love zebras! Did you know zebras have 7 mates, exactly 7 mates they service daily? Oh my, what a wonderful life!

22. STAR AND STRIPES

"Can you ride him?" I asked.

"Stevie from Cloudy Sky's used to be with the circus! He raised him. He's part of the Tranny Family!" said Tommy.

"His name is Fruit Loops! It goes with a line of zebra stripes, rainbow boot line Stevie is releasing this year," said MnMs.

"Fruit Boots!"

"He's friendly, doesn't need a saddle. Here's a step stool; hop on!" said Tommy D.

"One more thing, my nigga!" said MnMs.

MnMs tossed me a box. I opened it, and there were two of the most beautiful rings I had ever seen... Big Ass Diamonds!

"I don't know what to say, MnMs," I said.

"Thank you for saving the show, David. Can't have my nigga asking a young lady like Suzanna to marry you without proper bling-bling!" said MnMs.

"Thank you all... You're truly my friends," I said.

"Suzanna, will you marry me?" I asked, as I offered the bling-bling.

"Yes, David!"

"Now, will you ride on a zebra with me across Vegas to this meeting?" I asked.

"Yes! David, yes!" she said.

We hopped on the zebra! Believe it or not, he was well-behaved.

We got there quick as hell! Those fuckers are fast. Guess you gotta be when you've got lions and shit chasing you all the time!

As we arrived, Aila was waiting. Fuck, she looked pissed!

"What took you so long? The meeting is in 5 minutes!" Aila said.

"You have no idea," I said.
"Is that a zebra?" Aila asked.
"Yeah," I said.
"Who the fuck is she?" Aila asked.
"Suzanna... Aila... Aila... Suzanna," I said.
"Nice to meet you," said Suzanna.

"Yeah, you too... Let's go. Tie that animal up around the side so it doesn't freak people out!" said Aila.

"Damn, all my shit was jacked in L.A. in the Limo Bentley," I told Aila.

"Limo Bentley?" asked Aila.

"Don't ask," I said.

"I have it on my laptop," said Aila.

She licked her hand and wiped my hair down. Weird. Then I went in.

Well, it went great! They signed me for a multiple book deal! We all went to Tranny-Con, and it was a great success! Me and Suzanna got married at the Elvis Chapel, all thanks to the:

"Mother Fuckin' Tranny's on a Train!"

ABOUT THE AUTHOR

J

immy Swagger.... He was born in Alaska. Lived till he moved to Arkansas. He spent most of his years in the country. A real American hillbilly. He gathered his education in electrical engineering. He went onto work as an engineer and electrician. He had a wife at young age who passed away from breast cancer. He moved to Arizona and remarried. She was a good woman just indifferent.

They had 2 children. In the deterioration of this marriage he started to drink alcohol heavily. Destroying it more. They divorced and he was now onto clothing company also an electrical business. While riding the waves of depression he partnered into a recording company. He met another woman and she became very ill also. While hospital could fix her they discovered she had multiple sclerosis. She had a fall and was a paralyzed. She left hospital they discovered she was pregnant with a miracle baby. Well they moved to Michigan after getting indited by the FBI. He became incarcerated for some time. He discovered writing while behind bars. This began his new journey as an author.

SEE YOU SOON

Milton Keynes UK
Ingram Content Group UK Ltd.
UKHW030915121124
451094UK00001B/40

9 798227 488879